CLOWN FISH

By Rachel Rose

Consultant: Darin Collins, DVM
Director, Animal Health Programs, Woodland Park Zoo

BEARPORT
PUBLISHING

Minneapolis, Minnesota

Credits

Cover and title page, © Alex Stemmer/Shutterstock; 3, © cbpix/Shutterstock; 4–5, © BYONDJ/Alamy; 6, © Arunee Rodloy/Shutterstock, © michaelgeyer_photography/Shutterstock; 7, © Maxim Petrichuk/Shutterstock; 8–9, © Magnus Larsson/iStock; 11, © cbpix/Shutterstock; 13, © iStock/JodiJacobson; 14, © Tunatura/Shutterstock; 15, © tunart/iStock; 16, © optionm/iStock; 17, © ullstein bild/Getty; 19, © agus fitriyanto/Getty; 20-21, © Nature Picture Library/Alamy; 23, © FGorgun/iStock

President: Jen Jenson
Director of Product Development: Spencer Brinker
Senior Editor: Allison Juda
Associate Editor: Charly Haley
Designer: Colin O'Dea

Library of Congress Cataloging-in-Publication Data

Names: Rose, Rachel, 1968- author.
Title: Clown fish / by Rachel Rose.
Description: Minneapolis, Minnesota : Bearport Publishing Company, [2022] |
    Series: Library of awesome animals | Includes bibliographical references
    and index.
Identifiers: LCCN 2021002676 (print) | LCCN 2021002677 (ebook) | ISBN
    9781636911434 (library binding) | ISBN 9781636911519 (paperback) | ISBN
    9781636911595 (ebook)
Subjects: LCSH: Anemonefishes--Juvenile literature. |
    Anemonefishes--Ecology--Juvenile literature. | Coral reef
    fishes--Juvenile literature.
Classification: LCC QL638.P77 R67 2022 (print) | LCC QL638.P77 (ebook) |
    DDC 597/.72--dc23
LC record available at https://lccn.loc.gov/2021002676
LC ebook record available at https://lccn.loc.gov/2021002677

For more information, write to Bearport Publishing, 5357 Penn Avenue South, Minneapolis, MN 55419.
Printed in the United States of America.

Contents

AWESOME
Clown Fish!

WHOOSH, WHOOSH!
Two colorful clown fish wave their fins as they dart from side to side. With their bright bodies and wiggly ways, clown fish are awesome.

CLOWN FISH SWIM IN SHORT BURSTS IN A WAY THAT CAN MAKE THEM LOOK AS THOUGH THEY ARE BOUNCING.

True or False?

There are many kinds of clown fish. The most well-known are the true clown fish and the false clown fish, which are both bright orange. But clown fish can come in many colors. Most clown fish have white stripes. The pattern is what gives them their name because some say it makes the fish look like clowns.

A true clown fish

A false clown fish

CLOWN FISH CAN BE RED, PINK, YELLOW, BLACK, OR A MIX OF COLORS.

Home Sweet Home

These colorful fish live in the warm, **shallow** waters of the Indian and Pacific oceans, where there are plenty of **coral reefs**. Clown fish make their homes in sea anemones (uh-NEM-uh-neez) on the reefs. Anemones may look like plants, but they are actually animals with long tube-shaped **tentacles**. Clown fish spend most of their time living among the tentacles.

Best Buddies

They may make cozy clown fish homes, but sea anemone tentacles can sting anything that comes near. *YIKES!* Luckily, clown fish are covered in a **mucus** that protects them from the sting. In fact, clown fish and sea anemones have a great friendship. The fish stay safe as they hide among the tentacles. Clown fish also feed on any scraps left over from the anemones' meals.

CLOWN FISH AND ANEMONES ARE SO CONNECTED THAT CLOWN FISH ARE ALSO KNOWN AS ANEMONEFISH.

Two-Way Street

Sea anemones get something back for giving clown fish a safe home. Clown fish eat **parasites** that could harm anemones. They also clean up by eating dead anemone tentacles.

But even more importantly, clown fish help anemones eat and grow strong. The colors of the clown fish draw the anemones' **prey** close enough for the stinging tentacles to do their work.

Hide-and-Seek

The bigger the sea anemone, the safer the clown fish. Hiding among lots of tentacles keeps the small fish safe from stingrays, sharks, eels, and other **predators**.

But the biggest danger to clown fish is humans. More than one million clown fish are taken from the sea every year to be sold as pets.

ANOTHER DANGER TO CLOWN FISH IS POLLUTION IN THE OCEANS.

Egg-cellent Protection

The clown fish's anemone home even keeps fish babies safe. Clown fish **mate** a few times every year. **Females** lay hundreds—or even thousands—of eggs close to the anemones they call home. Then, the **males** look after the eggs until they **hatch** about a week later.

CLOWN FISH EGGS CAN ONLY HATCH AT NIGHT WHEN IT'S DARK.

Clown fish eggs

Oh Boy!

All clown fish start their lives as male. The young fish become part of a family group called a school. One female is at the head of each school. If the female dies, the biggest male in the group turns into a female. **PRESTO!** Once a male clown fish has turned into a female, it cannot turn back again.

> CLOWN FISH SCHOOLS STICK TOGETHER. THEY GUARD THEIR HOMES FROM OTHER CLOWN FISH.

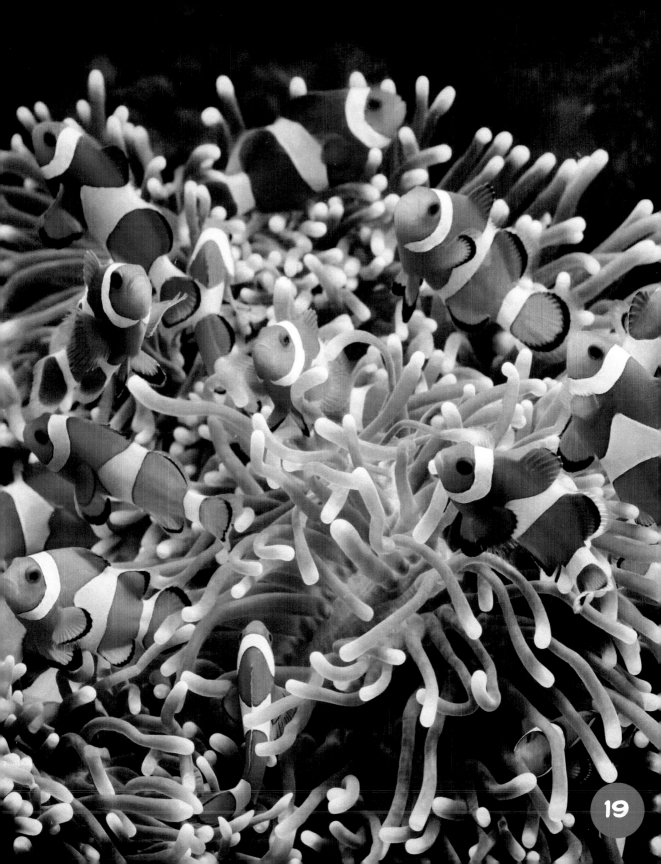

Girls Rule!

It can take young clown fish up to three years to become fully grown. And even then, they don't grow to be very big. The female clown fish is by far the largest in the school. Before a clown fish turns from male to female, it will get bigger. Now, that's awesome!

CLOWN FISH CAN LIVE FOR UP TO 10 YEARS.

CLOWN FISH ARE AWESOME!
LET'S LEARN EVEN MORE ABOUT THEM.

Kind of animal: Clown fish are fish. Like all fish, they are cold-blooded animals that breathe with gills.

More clown fish: There are 30 **species** of clown fish. Some scientists think there may be even more kinds that haven't been found yet.

Size: The largest clown fish can be up to 6 inches (15 cm) long. That's as long as a U.S. dollar bill!

CLOWN FISH AROUND THE WORLD

Arctic Ocean

NORTH AMERICA

EUROPE

ASIA

Pacific Ocean

Atlantic Ocean

AFRICA

Indian Ocean

Pacific Ocean

N W E S

SOUTH AMERICA

AUSTRALIA

WHERE CLOWN FISH LIVE

Southern Ocean

ANTARCTICA

Glossary

coral reefs rocklike structures formed from the skeletons of sea animals called polyps

females clown fish that can lay eggs

hatch to come out of an egg

males clown fish that cannot lay eggs

mate to come together in order to have young

mucus a slimy liquid made by an animal

parasites plants or animals that get food by living on or in another plant or animal

predators animals that hunt and kill other animals for food

prey animals that are hunted and eaten by other animals

shallow not very deep

species groups that animals and plants are divided into according to similar characteristics

tentacles long, armlike body parts used by some animals for moving, feeling, grasping, or stinging

Index

Read More

Kenney, Karen Latchana. *Fish Schools (Better Together: Animal Groups)*. Minneapolis: Jump! 2020.

Schuetz, Kari. *Clownfish and Sea Anemones (Blastoff! Readers: Animal Tag Teams)*. Minneapolis: Bellwether Media, 2019.

Learn More Online

1. Go to **www.factsurfer.com**
2. Enter "**Clown Fish**" into the search box.
3. Click on the cover of this book to see a list of websites.

About the Author

Rachel Rose writes books for children and teaches yoga. She lives in San Francisco with her husband and her dog, Sandy.